My Friend Rabbit

ERIC ROHMANN

ROARING BROOK PRESS

Brookfield, Connecticut

For Nicholas, Ethan, and William

Copyright © 2002 by Eric Rohmann   Published by Roaring Brook Press, a division of The Millbrook Press, 2 Old New Milford Road, Brookfield, Connecticut 06804   All rights reserved
Library of Congress Cataloging-in-Publication Data   Rohmann, Eric.   My friend rabbit / by Eric Rohmann.—1st ed.   p.   cm.   Summary: Something always seems to go wrong when Rabbit is around, but Mouse lets him play with his toy plane anyway because he is a good friend.
[1. Friendship—Fiction. 2. Rabbits—Fiction. 3. Mice—Fiction.] I. Title.   PZ7.R6413 My 2002   2002017764   [E]—dc21
ISBN 0-7613-1535-7 (trade edition)   10 9 8 7 6 5 4 3 2 1
ISBN 0-7613-2420-8 (library binding)   10 9 8 7 6 5 4 3 2 1
Printed in the United States of America   First edition

My friend Rabbit means well.
But whatever he does,
wherever he goes,

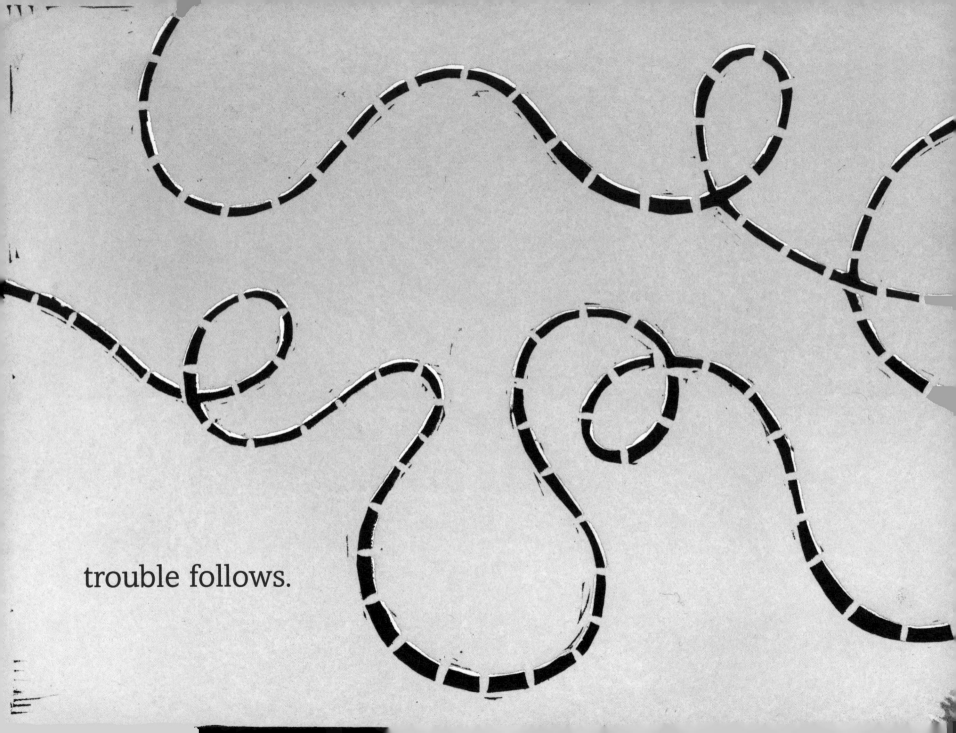

trouble follows.

"Not to worry, Mouse. I've got an idea!"

The plane was
just out of reach.
Rabbit said,
'Not to worry,
Mouse, I've
got an idea.'

So Rabbit held Squirrel
and Squirrel held me . . .

but then . . .

The animals
were not
happy.

But Rabbit means well.

And he is my friend.

Even if, whatever he does,

Rabbit, stop hugging me!

Thank you, Mouse!

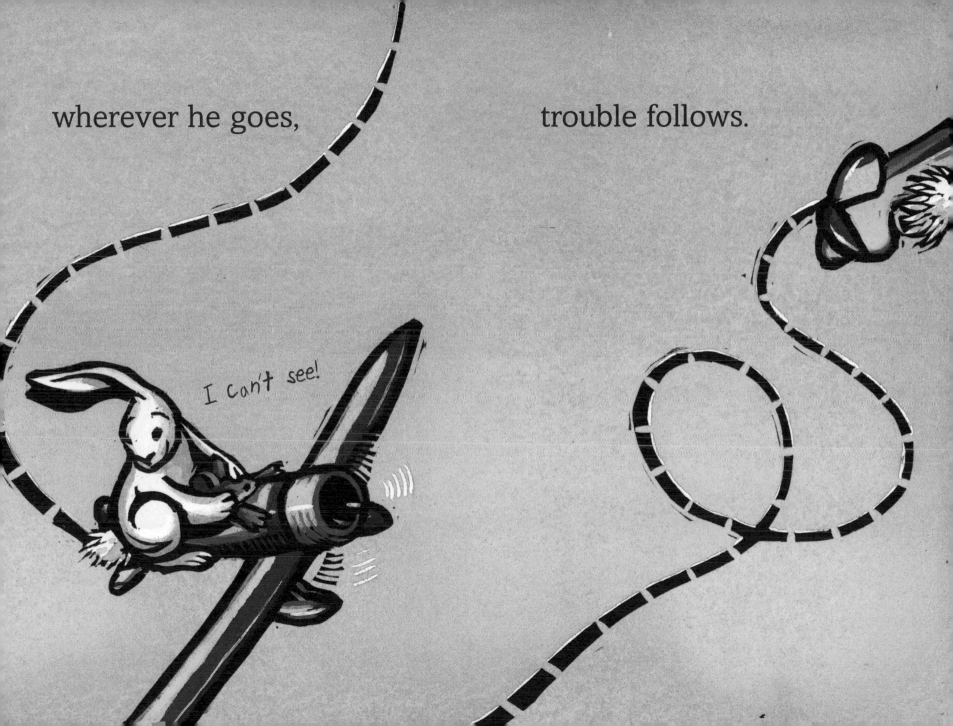

"Not to worry, Mouse,
I've got an idea."